TO
OLIVER,

From

....

You may have heard the stories?
I tell you they are true!
A superhero lives nearby.
But where? I wish I knew!

He's got an "O" upon his suit,
His cape is long and flowing.

Who is the boy behind the mask?
There's just no way of knowing!

They say he's very clever.
He's brave and fast and strong.
Do you know who he is yet?
His name's SIX letters long!

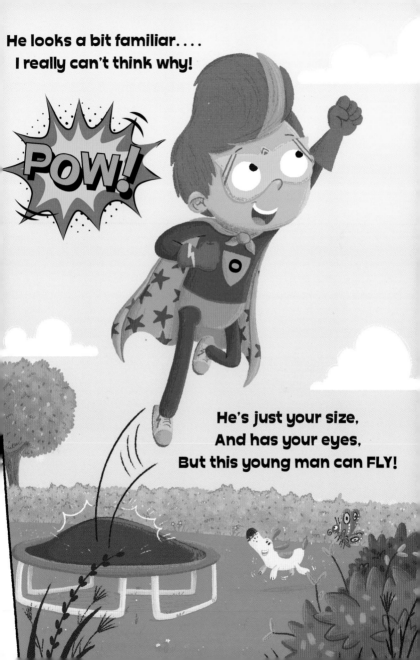

Oh no! A cat's stuck up a tree!
But who will get it out?
Our hero stops and says,
            "I'll use my. . .

SUPER
OLIVER
SHOUT!!!"

This little girl is crying.
Her trike has got a flat.

I guess it must be hungry work
When one is fighting crime.
He runs and jumps and dives around.
He's moving all the time!

Super Oliver's so strong,
He simply can't be beaten.
It must be all the salad, sprouts,
And broccoli he's eaten!

There's trouble on the playground!
Kids start to scream and shout.

Super Oliver will know
Just how to work this out!

Uh-oh! That child's about to fall.
He'll get a nasty scrape!

But never fear,
For guess who's here?
Our hero in a cape!

There's danger in the library!
That bookshelf looks too fragile.

He's the world's best superhero.
And he's got a super cuddle!

The next time you're in trouble,
Or ever in harm's way, shout...

This superhero stuff's hard work,
And now he's very sleepy,
But Super Oliver's afraid—
His bedroom looks so creepy!

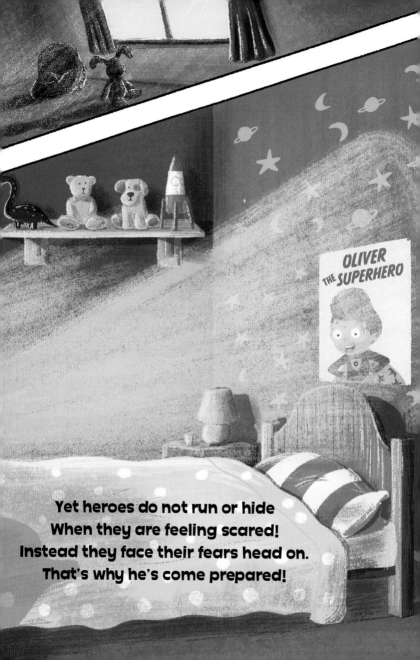

Yet heroes do not run or hide
When they are feeling scared!
Instead they face their fears head on.
That's why he's come prepared!

He's caring and he's helpful,
Always doing awesome deeds.
Super Oliver's the hero
Everybody needs!

He's always super-wonderful.
He's super-terrific, too.
Just who is Super Oliver?
I think it must be. . .

Written by Eric James
Illustrated by Steve Brown
Designed by Ryan Dunn

Published by Put Me In The Story,
a publication of Sourcebooks, Inc.
P.O. Box 4410, Naperville, Illinois 60567-4410
(630) 961-3900
www.putmeinthestory.com

Date of Production: October 2018
Run Number: HTW_PO201833
Printed and bound in Italy (LG)
10 9 8 7 6 5 4 3 2 1

put *me*
in the **story**®
Bestselling books starring your child!
www.putmeinthestory.com